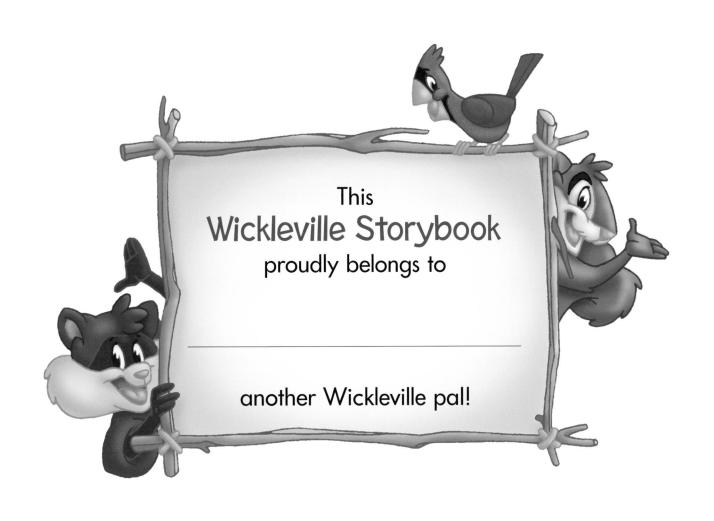

This
Wickleville Storybook
proudly belongs to

_____

another Wickleville pal!

Will Walter Ever Win?
©2000 by TREND enterprises, Inc.
Wickleville Woods™ is a trademark of TREND enterprises, Inc.

Printed in the United States of America

Lynae Wingate, John R. Kober – Editors

Library of Congress Catalog Card Number: 99-69469

ISBN 1-889319-77-5

10 9 8 7 6 5 4 3 2

Will Walter Ever Win?

by Jeffrey Sculthorp

Illustrations by Lorin Walter

WICKLEVILLE WOODS

TREND enterprises, Inc.

Every day after school, Walter the dog

played a game with his friend, Peeper the frog.

Some days they'd play hopscotch in Wickleville Park,

or play hide-and-go-seek until it was dark.

4

Other days they would see who could make the biggest mess. . .

And when they got bored, they played checkers or chess.

One day they decided to play tag—just for fun.

One would be frozen while the other would run.

Whichever game it was, whatever they'd choose,

it always seemed certain that Walter would lose.

Walter lost every game the two of them played,

including who could
sell the most lemonade!

14

One day Walter **almost** won his first race in years,

but right at the finish he tripped over his ears.

Losing to Peeper was always the same.

Walter said "Stop! No more playing those games."

Walter sat in his house for over 10 days,

not losing at all, in the usual ways.

Walter didn't want to play games ever again.

He was tired of losing to Peeper his friend.

But then Walter got
so lonely and sad.

He missed Peeper and the fun that they had.

24

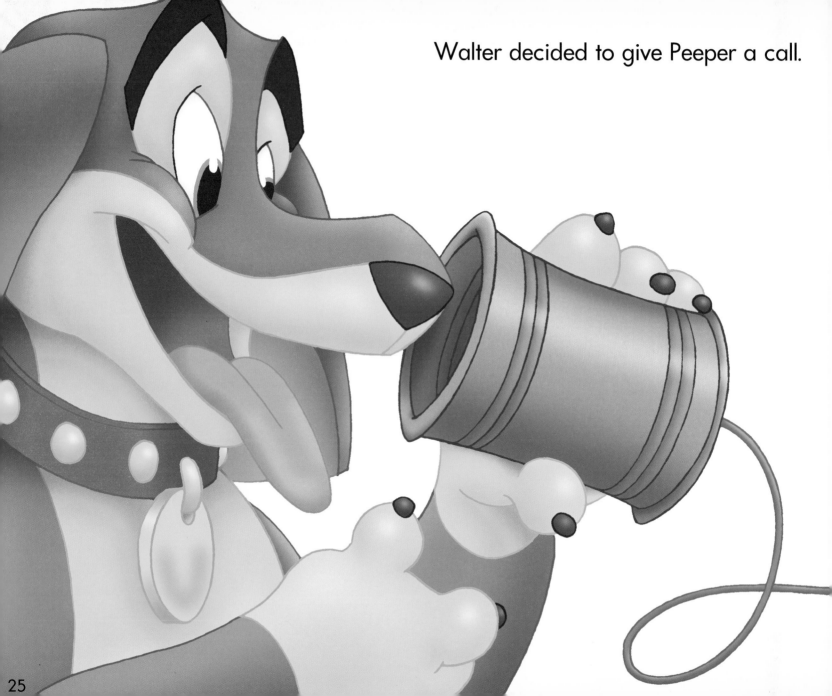

Walter decided to give Peeper a call.

25

Losing was better than not playing at all.

They raced together again; they both really tried.

When they reached the finish line, the two best friends tied.

28

The
End